DISCARD

Land of Yesterday, Land of Tomorrow

DISCOVERING CHINESE CENTRAL ASIA

Land of Yesterday, Land of Tomorrow

DISCOVERING CHINESE CENTRAL ASIA

PHOTOGRAPHS BY
Paul, David and Peter Conklin

TEXT BY
Brent Ashabranner

COBBLEHILL BOOKS / DUTTON
New York

To

Stephen Chicoine

Text copyright © 1992 by Brent Ashabranner
Photographs copyright © 1992 by Paul, David, and Peter Conklin
All rights reserved. No part of this book may be reproduced in any
form without permission in writing from the Publisher.

Library of Congress Cataloging-in-Publication Data
Conklin, Paul.
  Land of yesterday, land of tomorrow : discovering Chinese Central
Asia / photographs by Paul, David, and Peter Conklin ; text by Brent
Ashabranner.
      p.   cm.
  Includes bibliographical references (p.   ) and index.
  Summary: Photographs and text explore the Chinese province of
Xinjiang, closed to foreigners by the Communist government in 1949
and only reopened in 1984.
    ISBN 0-525-65086-5
    1. Sinkiang Uighur Autonomous Region (China) — Description and
travel — Juvenile literature.   [1. Sinkiang Uighur Autonomous Region
(China) — Description and travel.   2. China — Description and travel.]
I. Conklin, David, ill.   II. Conklin, Peter, ill.   III. Ashabranner,
Brent K., date.   IV. Title.
DS793.S62C66   1992
951'.6 — dc20   91-25145   CIP   AC

Published in the United States by Cobblehill Books, an affiliate of
Dutton Children's Books, a division of Penguin Books USA Inc.,
375 Hudson Street, New York, New York 10014
Designed by Charlotte Staub
Printed in Hong Kong
First Edition   10 9 8 7 6 5 4 3 2 1

Contents

Photographer's Note *ix*

Author's Note *xi*

ONE: Beyond China's Heartland 3

TWO: On the Silk Road 13

THREE: Dust and Photography on the Silk Road 23

FOUR: The Desert of Death and Living Oases 31

FIVE: People of China's Wild West 47

SIX: Kashgar 63

SEVEN: Land of Yesterday, Land of Tomorrow 77

Bibliography 81

Index 82

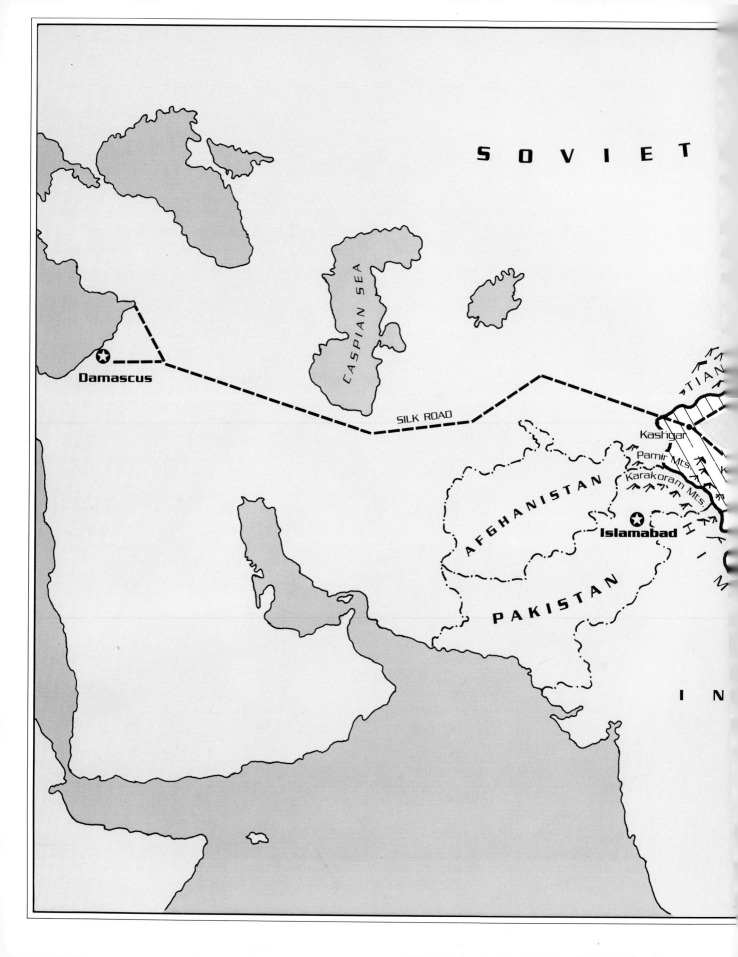

A Note on Spellings

The English spelling of some Chinese place names has not been standardized. For example, Taklamakan is spelled Takla Makan and Taklimakan in some atlases and other reference books. Xinjiang is sometimes spelled Sinjiang, Turpan sometimes Turfan. Tian Shan (Celestial or Heavenly Mountains) is often spelled Tien Shan or Tianshan. I have chosen the spellings that I believe to be in the most general use.

Brent Ashabranner

The quotation on page 34 is from *The Travels of Marco Polo* translated by Ronald Latham (Penguin Classics, 1958), copyright © Ronald Latham, 1958. Reproduced by permission of Penguin Books Ltd., Harmondsworth, Middlesex, England.

Photographer's Note

I am a professional photographer, and my cameras have been leading me to out-of-the-way places for almost as long as I can remember. For a working lifetime I have photographed people in fascinating and often remote parts of the world, trying, not always with success, to capture what is special about them, their lives, their surroundings.

I have walked with a Navajo boy across an arid corner of northern Arizona as he took the family sheep to a watering spot. I have stood at the top of a coal pit in a Welsh village and watched a shift of begrimed, weary miners come up after their long stay underground. I have followed a young Palestinian Arab boy and his father through a maze of alleyways in the old city of Jerusalem as they shopped for food for supper. These have been quiet adventures which have enriched my life.

On some of my travels I have been accompanied by my two sons, David and Peter. Inevitably during their passage from boys to young men they have been bitten by the photography bug. They could hardly have escaped the bite. David has become an accomplished photographer. He covered many of his expenses at the University of Iowa with his camera and is now a full-time photographer with his own studio in a small town in eastern Iowa. Peter was slower in feeling the lure of the camera and was almost through his college program in computer science before he enrolled in his first course in photography. His progress since then has been rapid.

Even though they are two years apart in age, Peter and David managed to graduate from college on the same day. Three months later we left on a trip that I had promised would be a celebration of their tenacity and hard work. We joined a small group of Smithsonian Institution Associates headed for China, but our destination was not such familiar tourist magnets as Shanghai and Beijing. Instead, we were going to the remote northwest of China—the province of Xinjiang—which had been closed to foreigners by the Chinese Communist government in 1949 and reopened only in 1984. Our group would be among the first Western visitors to this little-known part of China in over three decades.

In the pages ahead you will see the people and the country as we saw them through the eyes of our cameras.

Paul Conklin

Author's Note

$\mathcal{I}$ first met Paul Conklin in West Africa thirty years ago. He was an adventurous young free-lance photographer learning to make a living with his camera, and I was in charge of the Peace Corps program in Nigeria. In the years that followed we kept in touch and during the past decade have collaborated on ten books. Our subjects have ranged from America's everyday heroes in *People Who Make a Difference* to the plight of migrant farmworkers in *Dark Harvest*.

Paul asked me to write the text for this book and I agreed because by doing so I could in a small way share in the Conklin journey of discovery. Their photographs and notes were my principal writing guides. My research sources are listed in the bibliography. I wish to acknowledge the considerable help that I received from my friend Stephen Chicoine, whose research on and travel in Central Asia have made him a keen student of that fascinating part of the world.

Brent Ashabranner

Land of Yesterday, Land of Tomorrow

DISCOVERING CHINESE CENTRAL ASIA

A portion of the Great Wall of China near Beijing. Construction of this monumental forti-
fication began in the third century B.C., but much of it was built during the Ming dynasty
(1368–1644). Now largely in ruins, the Great Wall was only a partial success in keeping
out invading hordes of Mongol warriors.

ONE

Beyond China's Heartland

To some, it would have seemed a strange college graduation present that Paul Conklin had planned for his sons, David and Peter: a trip to one of the most remote, desolate, comfortless parts of the earth, a place of stark deserts, infrequent oases, rugged mountains, and raging sandstorms.

From another point of view, it was the opportunity of a lifetime: a chance to see a part of Chinese Central Asia little known to the Western world, long cloaked in mystery and legend; route of the ancient Silk Road over which Chinese goods first reached Persia, India, and Europe and products and ideas from those parts of the world entered China; a land of fiercely independent Muslim traders, nomads, and oasis dwellers who speak Turkic languages and look not at all like the Han Chinese

The bleak fringe of the Taklamakan Desert.

who make up most of the country's population. And the Conklins would visit Kashgar, a two-thousand-year-old city where Marco Polo had paused in his thirteenth-century journey to the court of the fabled Mongol ruler, Kublai Khan.

Paul thought that he knew his sons well enough to be sure that such a trip as a graduation gift would please them. And Paul was right. As quickly as they could wind up their college business, David and Peter packed their bags and cameras and were ready to travel.

The People's Republic of China is a giant, the third largest country in the world; only the Soviet Union and Canada are larger. China today stretches for 2,500 miles from the Pacific Ocean in the east to the Soviet border in the west. From its farthest northern border — also with the

Soviet—to its southern border with Vietnam, Laos, and Burma, the distance is some 2,000 miles. China's total land area is over 3.5 million square miles.

Within these far-flung borders lie the provinces that are often referred to as China Proper, the heartland that evolved from the great civilization that arose on the North China Plain thousands of years ago. The heartland is an area of 1.5 million square miles bounded on the north by the Great Wall, which extends from Gansu Province to the Yellow Sea. On the south the heartland is shielded by mountains and tropical forests; on the west by the Tibetan Plateau and desert wastelands; on the east by the Pacific Ocean. This is the historic homeland, the ancestral home, of the Chinese people who call themselves Han.

A heartland farmer.

The Han make up 93 percent of China's population of well over one billion people.

Surrounding this heartland and still within the borders of China are several huge, sparsely populated areas called "autonomous regions." Three of the largest and most important of these are the Inner Mongolia Autonomous Region, the Tibet Autonomous Region, and the Xinjiang Uighur Autonomous Region. (Xinjiang is pronounced shin-je-ang; Uighur is pronounced wee-gur). Since ancient times China has controlled these territories whenever it had the military and political means to do so. The Chinese have had many reasons for wanting these areas to be a part of China: to serve as a buffer against traditional enemies, to provide a source of minerals and other resources, to offer an outlet for Chinese products. The word "autonomous" suggests that these regions are permitted a good deal of self-rule; in fact, they are firmly a part of the People's Republic of China and have almost no independence from central government control.

The Conklins' destination was Xinjiang, the largest and westernmost of China's provinces. Xinjiang bears no resemblance, either in land or people, to the heavily populated, grain-growing heartland of China. Geographically and historically Xinjiang is a part of Central Asia long known as Turkestan, a vast area of plains, mountains, and deserts extending from the Caspian Sea where Europe and Asia meet to the Gobi Desert of Northern China and Mongolia. Turkestan has been inhabited for thousands of years by many tribes or culture groups of Turkic-speaking people. To the west this immense region has been known throughout much of history as Russian Turkestan, to the east as Chinese Turkestan.

With an area of 639,000 square miles Xinjiang is huge: three-fourths

Uighur woman. The Uighurs are citizens of China but bear little resemblance to the Han Chinese.

the size of the United States east of the Mississippi, four times the size of California. On every side nature has created a shield that for centuries made human penetration of Xinjiang an arduous and dangerous undertaking. On its northern border with the People's Republic of Mongolia rise the Altai Mountains; on the western border are the majestic Pamirs, called the Roof of the World because of peaks that soar to over twenty thousand feet; in the south the Kunlun Range forms the north wall of the Tibetan Plateau. Only on the eastern approach to Xinjiang are there no mountains, but from that direction the Gobi and Lop deserts for centuries presented travelers with problems as serious as those caused by mountains.

Has nature hidden a beautiful Shangri-La inside these formidable barriers of mountains and deserts? Hardly. The Tian Shan (Heavenly

Uighur man.

An elderly Han Chinese gentleman in Shanghai.

Mountains), beautiful but rugged, run eastward from the Pamirs, splitting the province. To the south of the Heavenly Mountains lies the Taklamakan Desert, which covers 135,000 square miles of Xinjiang Province and is considered to be one of the most dangerous deserts in the world.

The foothills of the Heavenly Mountains are covered with forests and pastures where nomadic Kazakh and Kirghiz tribesmen graze their flocks of sheep and goats and herds of horses and camels in the summer. Some rivers rising in the Kunlun, Pamir, and Altai mountain ranges form large but shallow lakes; other rivers disappear into the desert sands but still provide water for oases. Most of the land surrounding the Taklamakan is wasteland or semidesert which offers but meager forage for sheep, goats, and camels.

Until recent times the population of Xinjiang was made up mainly of Turkic-speaking people of different ethnic minority groups. By far the largest group are Uighurs—approximately 6 million—who have lived in this part of Central Asia since the ninth century. The Chinese government's official name for the province—Xinjiang Uighur Autonomous Region—recognizes both the Uighurs' numbers and historical place in the area. Smaller numbers of other ethnic minorities—Kazakhs, Kirghiz, Mongols, Tibetans, and others—also live in Xinjiang today. In recent years large numbers of Han Chinese have migrated to Xinjiang. The population of Xinjiang is about 15 million. This is only a little more than one percent of China's population of approximately 1,200,000,000, yet Xinjiang covers 20 percent of the country's total land area.

Historically, China wanted to control this part of Central Asia because it was a vital trade route. But today, when trade is carried out by giant ocean freighters and cargo aircraft, why would the Chinese

10

A group of Uighur men in Kashgar. The skullcaps are called *dopa* and are worn by Muslim men and women. They are often embroidered in bright colors.

government want such a poor region of desert and mountains? The answer lies partly in political geography. The Soviet Union, Pakistan, and Afghanistan are all on Xinjiang's western border. The deserts and mountains of this huge province provide a natural shield for the Chinese heartland that the government has every intention of maintaining.

Xinjiang is important to China for another reason, probably the most important reason of all. Exploration has shown that vast quantities of petroleum lie beneath the sands of the Tarim Basin; the basin is named for the Tarim River which rises in the Kunlun Mountains (between Tibet and Xinjiang) and winds its way around the northern edge of the Taklamakan Desert. The Tarim Basin is believed to be one of the largest untapped oil fields in the world, with reserves estimated as high as 18 billion tons. China's heartland oil fields are now maturing, and before many years production will decline. Then the oil of Xinjiang's Tarim Basin will be vital to China's development and economy.

In a very real sense, the future of China is buried beneath the sands of the Taklamakan Desert.

Camels near the Silk Road oasis of Dunhuang.

TWO

On the Silk Road

*T*he Conklins flew with their Smithsonian group from the United States to Beijing, the capital of the People's Republic of China. The group was made up of twenty-nine Smithsonian Associates of different professional backgrounds, but all had the same objective: to see and explore a part of western China and learn something about the historic Silk Road. Their travel and itinerary were arranged by the Smithsonian and the China Travel Service, with plenty of opportunity for individual exploration.

From Beijing the group flew to Xian (pronounced she-an) to catch the train that would carry them through Gansu Province and deep into Xinjiang. From the second century B.C., Xian, the ancient capital of China, was the beginning of the Silk Road for camel caravans traveling westward to India, Persia, and Europe. For traders arriving from those distant parts of the earth, Xian was the end of the perilous journey.

The train from Xian closely followed the route of the old Silk Road. On the second night out, Paul became convinced that trains in China must have square wheels. The train had a lurching, swaying motion and seemed to move ever more slowly as it crawled westward toward distant mountains. The rough ride, Paul concluded, was caused by a poorly built railbed or one that was badly in need of repair. From Paul, David, and Peter's point of view, the train's lack of speed was good because it gave them a better look at the countryside.

And despite the motion problems, train travel in China was proving to be fairly comfortable. They were in soft-sleeper class, which meant that they had a compartment with reasonably large beds, a small table for writing, and a lamp. There were even lace curtains and piped-in music. An attendant made sure that a Thermos of hot water for tea was in the compartment at all times and always well filled.

Most of the train was made up of hard-seat cars. Hard seat is the Chinese equivalent of second class; travelers were packed in tightly, and the cars were filled with tobacco smoke and food smells. People either brought food with them or bought it from vendors when the train stopped at a station. The hard seats were unpadded benches, and above them were several shelves on which passengers could sleep.

Paul, David, and Peter took their meals with the rest of their group in the dining car, eating mostly chicken and pork in stir-fried vegetables. From time to time when the train stopped, David supplemented their diet with moon cakes, which he bought from platform food vendors. They grew to like the round cakes (made to represent the full moon), although the sweet bean-paste filling took some getting used to.

The route of the Silk Road which the train now followed had been traveled by ancient caravans for fifteen hundred years with almost no deviation. The route's direction had been determined by one overriding consideration: the availability of water. Upon leaving Xian, caravans struck northwest for the Gobi Desert oasis of Dunhuang, a journey of several weeks. From there the objective was to reach the important oasis city of Kashgar where the caravans would rest, buy fresh camels, and acquire additional merchandise before crossing the dangerous Pamir and Karakoram mountains and beginning the long descent toward India or Persia. For many caravans the destination was Damascus, the marketplace at which East and West met. From Mediterranean ports merchandise would be shipped to Alexandria and Rome.

But the direct route from Dunhuang to Kashgar was blocked by the massive, waterless sand dunes of the Taklamakan Desert, a desert so forbidding that even birds will not attempt to fly over it. Upon leaving Dunhuang, caravans had the choice of circling to the north or south of the Taklamakan, stopping at oases that clung to the great desert's edge on either side. The northern route, which passed through the foothills of the Tian Shans, the Heavenly Mountains, was favored by most caravans. One reason for this was that it made possible a stop at the major oasis of Turpan. By either route, the goal was to reach Kashgar and regroup before ascending to the Roof of the World.

This great trade route was long and filled with peril; few accounts by early travelers fail to mention the bones of men and animals that littered the desert and mountain trails. On some parts of the route bandit gangs were a constant menace. The Jiayuguan fortress near Dunhuang marked the western end of the Great Wall of China. The fortress was one of the last reassuring sights for Silk Road travelers before they began their journey into the desert unknown.

A dramatic view of the Ming dynasty fortress near the town of Jiayuguan in Gansu Province. The Great Wall in this area is now only rubble, but the Jiayuguan fortress is still an imposing structure.

But at that time in history, before sea routes between Europe and the Orient were developed, only hazardous overland commerce was possible. Despite the danger, the potential of great financial reward tempted thousands of merchants over the centuries. The appetite of the outside world for Chinese goods knew no limits; China's desire for products from India, the Middle East, and Europe was just as great.

During the approximately fifteen hundred years that this great commercial highway was in use, hundreds of products and invaluable knowledge flowed in both directions. China-bound caravans carried gold, ivory, coral, asbestos, peaches, walnuts, spices, the art of glassmaking and glazing. A vastly superior breed of horse came from Arabia. Out of China came furs, iron, porcelain, gunpowder, lacquer, the art of papermaking and movable-type printing.

But from the first century A.D. and for several hundred years after that, the most highly prized commodity to be carried on the great East-West trade route was silk. The Byzantine Empire and Rome immediately fell under the spell of the new textile, so beautiful to look at, so delightful to touch. Romans loved to dress themselves in "glass togas," as they called garments made of the wondrous see-through material. The rage for silk was so great that it became a serious drain on the Roman treasury. Its price was frighteningly high; according to some historians, silk was sold for its exact weight in gold! That may have been an exaggeration, but there is no question that it was shockingly expensive.

Romans knew that silk came from a mysterious Eastern country, and they were convinced that the marvelous cloth grew on trees. The Chinese did and said nothing to cause them to think otherwise. The Chinese were the first people to make silk from the cocoons of the silkworm or *Bombyx mori* caterpillar, and for almost three thousand years only they knew how to make this beautiful textile. The Chinese closely guarded the secret of silkmaking; anyone who might have revealed the secret to the outside world would have faced disgrace and death. About 550 A.D., however, two Christian monks from Constantinople smuggled some silkworms out of China, and in time the Chinese monopoly on silk was lost.

The term "Silk Road" is not old; it was coined by the German geographer-scholar Ferdinand von Richtofen in the nineteenth century. But there could scarcely be a more fitting name for the trade route that linked China with the rest of the ancient world.

The most important importation into China over the Silk Road was not a commodity, however, not spices or precious metals or glass. Far more meaningful to the future of China and much of the rest of East

This elegant black Buddha, cast in bronze, was photographed by David in a Shanghai temple after the Silk Road trip.

Asia was an idea, a concept that arrived from India, probably sometime in the first century A.D. The new arrival was Buddhism, a religion born in India in the sixth century B.C. Buddhism's doctrines of morally right thinking and compassion for all living things found fertile ground in China, first taking hold around such important Silk Road oases as Turpan and Dunhuang. A great Buddhist monastery called Bezelik was built in the Flaming Mountains near Turpan in the ninth century. It became a treasury of Buddhist art, including hundreds of frescoes. For a thousand-year period between the fourth and fifteenth centuries, caves, called the Magao Caves, were dug into hills near Dunhuang to house Buddhist art. As Islam became the dominant religion of this part of Central Asia, the Bezelik monastery and the Magao Caves were

18

abandoned and became a part of the "lost" civilization of the Taklamakan region. Although a few fine frescoes remain, much of the art of
Bezelik and the Magao Caves was removed by European explorer-
adventurers early in the twentieth century.

But the Silk Road provided the avenue by which Buddhism found
its way into the Chinese heartland, Korea, Japan, and other parts of
the Orient, deeply affecting the life and art of much of Asia.

The abandoned Buddhist monastery of Bezelik in the Flaming Mountains near Turpan.

20

A view of the Magao Caves, storehouse of Buddhist art, near Dunhuang. Photograph by Susan Van Etten.

Dust is the enemy of every photographer. In Xinjiang there was no avoiding it.

THREE

Dust and Photography on the Silk Road

Dust is a part of life in China; it is everywhere: in the cities and villages, in the trains, on the roads, in the markets. One of Paul's first China memories is of women, wearing masks as they pushed long-handled brooms in the early-morning light, sweeping up the thick dust that settles in the capital city of Beijing every night.

As the train carried Paul, David, and Peter ever westward on the route of the Silk Road, across the edge of the Gobi Desert and along the fringe of the Taklamakan Desert, the dust became progressively worse. One of Paul's notes calls Dunhuang "the grit capital of the world." But when they reached Kashgar, he wrote the same thing about that old city, except that he called it "the dust capital of the universe."

In fact, the dust of China is different in different places. The fine, yellowish-brown dust that falls on Beijing is called loess (pronounced les or lō′es); it is a rich loam created thousands of years ago by dust and silt driven by cyclonic winds from the Gobi and Taklamakan deserts. Winnowed by the wind and deposited far beyond the desert, sometimes to thicknesses of two hundred or even three hundred feet in provinces such as Gansu and Shansi, loess is now China's richest farmland. In Dunhuang the air is full of grit blown from huge sand dunes that tower at the edge of the oasis. In Kashgar the dust is fine and powdery and hangs in clouds every time a truck or donkey cart rattles by; it permeates everything: luggage, beds, even tightly closed camera bags.

The technical distinctions between kinds of dust did not impress Paul; they were all a menace to a photographer. From experience in desert areas of the American Southwest, Peru, North Africa, and India, he knew that one grain of sand grit in the delicate mechanism of a camera could disable it. This is a working photographer's nightmare, for the camera is useless until it can be professionally cleaned — a service not likely to be found in the desert.

Paul's advice to desert photographers: keep your cameras in tightly sealed Ziploc bags when they are not being used. When they are being used, there is not much you can do but be as careful as possible. That means changing lenses as infrequently as possible, not pointing the camera directly into a strong wind unless you must to get an irresistible shot, keeping the cap on the lens except when shooting, and giving the camera as much protection with coat or shirt as feasible.

The other enemy of a photographer working in western China or any other desert area is heat. Film is perishable. Heat ruins it, and one of Paul's main concerns on the Silk Road was that their film not be cooked on an overheated bus or left in the sun in some sweltering

Sweeping dust (loess) from a sidewalk in Beijing. The woman repeats this task every morning.

market. The solution was to bring with them inexpensive insulated bags of the sort picnickers use and to keep all their film in them. The bags worked fine, and their chief problem then became not to lose them.

In one terrifying mental lapse in the airport of the Xinjiang capital of Urumqi (u-rum-chi), Paul left his camera bags at the check-in counter near the X-ray machine. Sometime later a concerned Chinese customs officer located Paul and handed him his bags. Paul had not been aware that he had wandered off without them.

Although he travels and works with several cameras, Paul's favorite is a fine old Leica, which he has had for years. On the China trip David

Children are usually ready to smile for the camera, just as these Uighur elementary school students were in Kashgar.

26

Student teachers in Kashgar. This picture shows just how open and unafraid Uighur women are today.

used mainly a Nikon and Peter a Canon. But on the subject of cameras and picture taking Paul has this to say:

"I have changed camera systems twice since the Silk Road trip, partly to go to automatic focus for the benefit of my middle-aged eyes. These changes have reinforced my belief that it doesn't matter much which cameras a person uses just as long as he is comfortable with them and understands them.

"More important than the kind of cameras and lenses — much more important — in western China (and most other places, for that matter), is how you approach the people you wish to photograph. Busy streets and markets usually present few problems. Use your cameras as discreetly and quietly as you can, attracting as little attention to yourself

"It's amazing how well you can communicate without using language," says Peter. Here he lets a new friend look through his camera on a Kashgar street.

as possible. If you see a person you wish to photograph, approach with a smile and a gesture which will make your intentions clear. If there is any resistance, *don't push*. Smile again and leave. There will always be other good pictures to take.

"Fortunately, most Uighurs seem to like being photographed. What a joy for the professional photographer!"

Early in the trip David learned the value of a smile. At one of the desert stops, he left the train to look around the station. At one end of the platform two Uighur men stared at him intently, speaking softly to each other. David summoned his courage and approached the two men. He smiled and touched the camera slung around his neck. After a moment the men returned his smile, and David got his picture.

Peter has many memories of the friendliness of the people. "It is amazing," he said, "how well you can communicate without sharing a language."

These young Uighur women at a Turpan textile factory were happy to have their picture taken.

Melons are one of the main products of the Taklamakan oases, and most markets have large mounds of them. This is a scene in the old section of Kashgar.

FOUR

The Desert of Death and Living Oases

The Sahara Desert in Africa is the largest desert on earth, larger than the continental United States. The Atacama Desert in Peru is the driest place on earth; not a drop of rainfall was recorded there during a twenty-one-year period between 1950 and 1971. But for thousands of years travelers, explorers, and geographers have agreed that the most evil desert on earth is the Taklamakan Desert of Chinese Central Asia. The very name is evil. Taklamakan is a Turkic word which means "if you go in, you won't come out."

The Swedish explorer Sven Hedin, who knew the Taklamakan well, spoke of it as "the worst and most dangerous desert in the world." Geographer Sir Percy Sykes called the Taklamakan "the Land of Death."

These descriptions are not exaggerations. History records the disappearance of entire caravans in the Taklamakan's wastelands. According to legend two armies are buried beneath the desert's sand dunes, some of which tower to six hundred feet — twice the length of a football field. For centuries legends also told of cities buried under the shifting, creeping sands of the Taklamakan. In some tales handed down from father to son among oasis dwellers, the number of cities buried, abandoned, or lost in the vast desert was said to be at least three hundred. In the early years of this century, several treasure-hunting Western archaeologist-adventurers proved that the legends were rooted in fact. They found several of the lost cities and carried off an enormous wealth of Buddhist art and manuscripts to the museums of Europe and the United States.

What has given the Taklamakan its evil reputation? In the first place, it is huge, almost the size of North Carolina, South Carolina, and Georgia combined; it blocks any direct overland route from Xian to Kashgar and from Kashgar to the heartland of China. Whether heading east or west caravans had to circle to the northern or southern fringes of the desert and struggle for weeks from one oasis to the next.

The Taklamakan is one of the driest of the earth's deserts, lying in a rain shadow on the leeward side of the Karakoram, Altai, and Kunlun mountain ranges. At certain times of the year the heat in the desert is terrible, often reaching 125 degrees. At other times the cold is equally terrible.

But of all the terrors of the Taklamakan, none can match the dreaded sandstorm that is known as *kara-buran* (black hurricane). The *kara-buran* forms with numbing swiftness, darkening the sky, bringing howling winds that drive sand and gravel with almost bullet force. The winds swirl madly, pushing tons of sand high into the sky, sending it crashing

32

Paul called the landscape around Turpan some of the bleakest he had ever seen. David captured that bleakness in this photograph taken in the Flaming Mountains near Turpan.

down on camels and their masters in caravans of yesterday, on oil-rig workers and sheepherders at the desert's edge today. As the *kara-buran* continues, the desert grows ever darker, and terrifying noises are added to the howling wind: noises that sound like the boom of distant cannons, a rushing locomotive, a great building collapsing. One traveler called the *kara-buran* a frenzy of nature "like hell let loose." Despite the heat, he said, a man could only wrap himself heavily in clothes or blankets and lie down until the fury passed, which might not be for hours or even days.

The most famous traveler ever to make his way over the Silk Road was Marco Polo. He sailed from Venice in the summer of 1271 with his father, Nicolo, and his uncle Maffeo, who were merchants; Nicolo and Maffeo had made one trip to China and decided to take Marco on their second voyage to the Orient. Marco was seventeen years old when they set sail for the Middle East. They reached Kashgar two years later traveling over the Silk Road from Persia, and Marco spent the next twenty years in China in the service of the great Mongol emperor Kublai Khan. After he returned to Venice in 1295, he wrote a book about his adventures, *The Travels of Marco Polo*, which astounded Europeans and is perhaps the greatest travel book of all time. Here are a few lines from his description of the Taklamakan Desert:

> . . . When a man is riding by night through this desert and something happens to make him loiter and lose touch with his companions . . . he hears spirits talking in such a way that they seem to be his companions. Sometimes, indeed, they even hail him by name. Often these voices make him stray from the path, so that he never finds it again. And in this way many travellers have been lost and have perished. And sometimes in the night they are conscious of a noise like the clatter of a great cavalcade of riders away from the road; and, believing that these are some of their own company, they go where they hear the noise, and when day breaks, find they are victims of an illusion and in an awkward plight. . . . Yes, and even by daylight men hear these spirit voices, and often you fancy you are listening to strains of many instruments, especially drums, and the clash of arms. For this reason bands of travellers make a point of keeping very close together. Before they go to sleep they set up a sign pointing in the direction in which they have to travel. And round the necks of all their beasts they fasten little bells, so that by listening to the sound they may prevent them from straying off the path.

All the strange sounds reported by Marco Polo have been heard by other travelers in the Taklamakan Desert, and all have been explained scientifically: sand cliffs collapsing, wind currents among the dunes, the shifting of the massive mountains of sand. Today we may believe that science has the correct answers, but Marco Polo was reporting what oasis dwellers of the Taklamakan region have believed for centuries: that demons or evil spirits live in the desert and lure men to dreadful death in the waterless wastelands.

In keeping with its dark reputation as a place of death, it seems fitting that the Chinese government has chosen the Taklamakan Desert as the testing grounds for its nuclear weapons.

The suddenness with which an oasis appears in the arid fringes of the Taklamakan is startling, even shocking. "You have been riding on a train or a bus for hours," Peter recalled. "You're almost in a trance

Putting up hay in a Han village near Urumqi.

A bicycle repairman in a Taklamakan oasis. Bicycles are an essential means of transportation everywhere in China.

from staring at the vast emptiness of western China. You've seen a few camels and now and then some sheep or goats, but they are just dots on the endless monochromatic landscape. And then—it seems like just in the time it takes you to blink—everything is green. There are trees and cornfields and melon patches and grapevines. There are people working in the fields, walking along the road, riding bicycles. Lots of people. It's like you're dreaming. It doesn't seem real."

But the oases of Xinjiang are real, and some of them are centuries old. About a thousand of these patches of green dot the vast north and south fringes of the Taklamakan, and the economy of the province depends on them. Most are small, just dusty villages of a few hundred people; but some — Turpan, Kucha, Kashgar, Khotan — are large enough to be called oasis cities. Urumqi, the capital of Xinjiang Province, is a relatively recent Han creation. With a population of almost one million, it is a major oasis city; it is a mixture of modern buildings, even skyscrapers, and good housing with crowded, run-down sections.

Most people think of an oasis as a desert pond or watering hole surrounded by palm trees. Such oases do exist, but in fact an oasis is any fertile area in a desert where there is enough water for a good deal of vegetation. Some oases spread out for miles and have extended and varied agricultural activity.

The key, of course, is water. The water which brings life to the oases of the Taklamakan region comes from rainwater and huge amounts

A shady lane in one of the Turpan oasis villages. Most houses in the Taklamakan oases are built of plastered-over mud bricks.

of melting snow from the surrounding mountains, some of which are close by, others far away. In some cases, reservoirs are built in nearby mountains, and water is brought to the oases through ordinary irrigation channels. In certain locations, deep irrigation wells are drilled—over six hundred in the Turpan area.

The most important way in which water is brought to the oases, however, is through a system of man-made underground channels called *karez* in the Uighur language. The *karez* is a remarkable engineering achievement, a technological marvel that allows water to move from the mountains to the oases through tunnels. *Karez* builders find a spring at the foot of a mountain where water gathers and soaks into the ground until it reaches the water-bearing stratum. Even though this stratum may be a hundred feet underground, it is still considerably higher than the oasis on the desert floor. Graded tunnels are dug to this mountain source, and water is guided to the oasis until it trickles out to irrigate the farmers' fields. Vertical shafts that connect with the tunnel are dug at regular intervals; men digging the tunnels get fresh air from the shafts, and the shafts are used for hauling dirt from the tunnels.

No one is certain how long *karez* have been dug in Xinjiang, but the idea came from Persia. Similar systems were known to have been in use there and other parts of the Middle East since biblical times. There is evidence that *karez* were dug in Chinese Central Asia as long as five hundred years ago and that their use increased during the Ching dynasty, which began in 1644.

Today almost two thousand miles of *karez* are in use in Xinjiang. In the oases, *karez*-building skills have been handed down from father to son in some families for generations. *Karez* workers have their own guilds or labor organizations and spend their lives building new *karez* and maintaining the old ones.

38

Entrance to a vertical shaft leading to a *karez* tunnel. Photograph by Stephen Chicoine.

In a Turpan carpet factory. Most of the larger oases have carpet factories, and carpets are also handwoven by villagers in their spare time. The carpets of Khotan, made from long, thick local wool, are especially prized, as are fine old Kashgar carpets.

40

After they left Dunhuang, the first major objective of caravans taking the northern route of the Silk Road was the oasis of Turpan. Centuries after the Silk Road fell into disuse, Turpan is still the first important stop for the train traveler to Xinjiang Province. The center of the oasis has shops and other buildings, a rug factory, and a market, but Turpan is really a collection of villages clustered around this center. The villages are tiny, in most cases no more than a few houses of an extended family; all are surrounded by melon patches, vineyards, and cottonfields and cornfields.

Corn has been grown in Turpan, as well as in many other Taklamakan oases, for centuries. Marco Polo tells how the oasis dwellers would hide their newly harvested corn in secret wasteland caves to keep passing armies, either enemy or friendly, from taking it.

Uighur children in a cornfield near Kashgar.

Roads in Turpan are lined with white poplar trees, and these trees are grown in other oases where *karez* water is plentiful. The fast-growing poplars have many uses. Their shade brings welcome coolness, and they serve as a windbreak and defense against the ever-encroaching desert. They provide valuable lumber and scraps become firewood. Poplar trees have been grown in Chinese Central Asia for centuries. Splintered trunks of poplars were found buried in the sand at Dandan-uilik, one of the "lost" cities of the Taklamakan.

Despite the wind and sandstorms that buffet Turpan, water from the *karez* and wells plus the heat have combined to make the Turpan area a virtual outdoor hothouse, not unlike the irrigated Imperial Valley of California. For centuries, Turpan has been well known for its vegetables and grain and even more famous for its grapes: sweet white

A happy Turpan resident brings home a turkey from the market. In the background are white poplar trees, which line the roads of many Taklamakan oases.

Grapes from a Turpan vineyard.

seedless grapes which are dried to make raisins and a large, juicy red grape called mare's milk, always eaten in its natural state. Most famous of all are the orange-fleshed musk melons, which are highly prized in other parts of China.

Other Taklamakan oases have their own specialties — peaches, pomegranates, figs, apricots — but all have one thing in common: their life-giving groundwater comes from the rain and snows of the mighty mountain ranges that surround them.

Open-air restaurants flourish in all good-sized Xinjiang oases and outnumber the indoor type by ten to one. Freshly made noodles are standard fare at almost every restaurant. In a process that has hardly changed over centuries, the cook kneads and stretches the dough, skillfully turning it into strands of noodles. Tradition holds that Marco Polo

Making noodles in an open-air restaurant.

An open-air restaurant in Kashgar.

took the art of noodle-making back to Venice. In time that original importation developed into spaghetti, fettucine, macaroni, and all the other delicious pastas that we enjoy today.

Paul, David, and Peter found some of the food in Xinjiang good. Watermelons and cantaloupes became a staple of their diets; they liked the small meat and onion pies called *kao baozi* and boiled stuffed dumplings filled with meat paste. Their breakfasts usually consisted of hot tea, bread, honey, and hard-boiled eggs. They ate a lot of scrambled eggs and tomatoes. Some foods they learned quickly to avoid: boiled sheep's head and fatty lung cooked in a hot, spicy oil.

Peter attended a dinner where a whole roasted sheep was served. The head was still on the sheep, and a red ribbon had been tied around its neck. "I didn't eat much," he said.

David and Peter were more adventurous than their father when it came to eating on the street.

45

The Wong family. Although most farmers in Xinjiang are Uighurs, some Han Chinese immigrants, like the Wongs, have become successful farmers.

FIVE

People of China's Wild West

It was a chance meeting on a dusty road outside Turpan. Paul was on foot, walking to get a better sense of the oasis. A farmer on a bicycle passed him. A solid, wide-bladed hoe was strapped to the back of the bicycle, which meant that the farmer was going to join other workers cultivating their small plots of land on either side of the road. It was the time of day to do hard work. Even though the season was fall, Turpan was still a patch of green in the arid Taklamakan fringe because of irrigation water from the *karez*. The morning air was cool, but by midday the temperature would be well over one hundred degrees.

Paul thought that the farmer was surely startled as he rode past. After all, tall Americans ladened with cameras must have been as common in that out-of-the-way corner of western China as grizzly bears are on the streets of Washington, D.C. Elsewhere in China foreign visitors have become frequent and do not attract much attention, but Paul was sure the farmer had never encountered anyone like him before.

Yet there was no flicker of surprise on the man's face. Instead, he smiled and beckoned for Paul to follow. A few minutes later Paul ducked through a doorway in a mud wall and found himself in the courtyard of the farmer's small house. They still had not exchanged a word. The farmer's wife sat on a stool in the middle of the courtyard, two children at her side, as she prepared a leafy vegetable for cooking. The children scrambled behind their mother, but she simply looked up at Paul and smiled. It was as if her husband brought home foreign strangers every day.

After a moment of silence, Paul haltingly tried some of the simple Chinese expressions he had learned before beginning the trip. They broke the ice. The woman brought Paul a slice of melon, which, he soon learned, seemed to be a universal expression of hospitality in rural Xinjiang. The farmer examined Paul's cameras with great interest, then he and his wife changed from their work clothes, and Paul took a family portrait.

They exchanged addresses. The farmer wrote in Chinese, and it was only when he found a translator that Paul learned the man's name was Wong. Paul said good-bye and continued his walk down the dusty road outside Turpan. It had been a warm, simple, friendly encounter.

Xinjiang has sometimes been called China's Wild West, and this implied comparison with America's Western frontier is not so farfetched. Besides the friendliness of the people that Paul found in Turpan and at other oases, the most obvious similarity is the land itself. Many times on their journey, the flat, arid landscape with distant mountains re-

Kazakhs are the traditional sheepherders of Xinjiang. Except for the rider's clothes and whip, this scene could be in New Mexico or Arizona.

A Kazakh family moves down from the foothills of the towering Tian Shan at the end of summer.

minded Paul of parts of Texas, New Mexico, Arizona, and southern California, as did the flocks of placid sheep that grazed under the watchful eyes of mounted herders. Although their systems of irrigation are very different, Xinjiang and the American Southwest are also similar in their use of groundwater to create farming areas in the desert.

Horses played an important role in the history of the American West, first for the Plains Indians in hunting buffalo, then as the means by which ranchers controlled vast herds of cattle on the range and in moving them to railroad shipping points. In Chinese Central Asia today horses are vital to Kazakhs (pronounced ka-zaks), a nomadic people who still follow the way of life of their ancestors. They are herders, using their horses to drive their flocks of sheep and goats to the lush foothill pastures of the Tian Shan and other mountains during the summer; in the fall they move their animals to lower ground. Kazakhs carry their houses, called *yurts*, and all other possessions with them as they move from place to place. A yurt is a rectangular tent of felt or skins stretched on four wooden lattice frames and poles. Although somewhat different in shape, a yurt is not unlike the tepee once used by American Indians.

Some Kazakh families have small herds of cattle, but their income is derived mainly from sheep. Milky tea, sun-dried cheese balls, and fried bread are staples of the Kazakh diet. They eat meat only on festive occasions such as weddings.

Young Kazakh men love to display their skill with horses in a game called *buz kashi*. In this game two teams of excellent horsemen compete for a prize — the carcass of a sheep whose head and insides have been removed. The first team that can grab the carcass and place it in a spot that has been designated as the goal is the winner. *Buz kashi*, which probably dates from the thirteenth century, echoes a time when warriors

Kazakh men playing *buz kashi*. The rider at the center has control of the sheep carcass, but the other team will try to snatch it away from him before he reaches the goal.

of one tribe would raid an enemy tribe, carrying off sheep, camels, and other plunder. *Buz kashi* is a violent game in which riders are sometimes killed, but it is a popular sport at Kazakh festivals.

With a population of about one million, Kazakhs are the second-largest minority in Xinjiang Province. The main body of the Kazakh people — about 7 million — are citizens of the Soviet Union and live in the Kazakh Soviet Socialist Republic. While some Kazakhs migrated to Chinese Central Asia as early as the thirteenth century, large numbers fled to Xinjiang during the 1930s rather than submit to the Communist system of the collective control of property. Although China is also a Communist country, the Kazakhs living in Xinjiang have continued their old ways of individual ownership of their horses, sheep, and other animals. Kazakhs, both in Xinjiang and the Soviet Union have continued to practice the Muslim faith through the years despite efforts of authorities to discourage them.

Although Han Chinese make up most of the country's population, the Chinese government recognizes fifty-five ethnic minorities totalling more than 60 million people. With about 6 million, the Uighurs are the third largest ethnic minority in China and by far the largest of the thirteen different minority culture groups living in Xinjiang today. Other minorities such as the Kazakhs, Mongolians, Kirghiz (nomads like the Kazakh), Daur, Xibe, and Tajik make up less than 10 percent of Xinjiang's total population.

Originally from western Turkestan, Uighurs moved east in the seventh century, conquering Mongolia. They were forced out of Mongolia in 840 by another Turkic tribe, the Kirghiz, and driven westward. The Uighurs established an empire in Xinjiang late in the ninth century; since that time, for over a thousand years, this part of Central Asia has been their home. At times during that long span of history, the Uighurs have fallen under the rule of other people such as the Mongols in the thirteenth century and the Chinese at different times. Since the middle of the seventeenth century, Xinjiang has been politically a part of China, and all Uighurs living in Xinjiang Province are citizens of China.

But they do not consider themselves Chinese. In the face of all political changes and outside pressures, Uighurs have stubbornly held

Young Kazakh women in festive dress watch a
game of *buz kashi*. All Kazakh children are trained
from an early age to be good riders.

The faithful pray at Id Kah mosque in Kashgar. Almost all Uighurs are Muslims, as are many of the other Xinjiang minorities such as Kazakhs and Kirghiz.

56

onto their religion, language, customs, and ways of making a living.

In the tenth century Uighurs converted to the relatively new faith of Islam brought to eastern Central Asia by Arab traders and armies; for a thousand years they have remained faithful Muslims. China's powerful central government has made Chinese language study important in Xinjiang schools, but Uighurs have clung fiercely to their own language. Uighur is still the most widely spoken language in Xinjiang and is almost exclusively the language of trade in the markets. Early in their migration to Xinjiang, Uighurs gained control of the oases in the region and became farmers. They have remained farmers over the centuries and have become well known throughout China for their fine fruits, particularly grapes and melons. In the days of the Silk Road the main oases of Xinjiang became important markets; Uighurs developed their skills as traders and to this day dominate the markets and bazaars of the Xinjiang oasis cities.

Most Uighurs are eager for their children to get an education, but many parents cannot afford even the low fees that the schools must charge. Chinese schools—including those in Xinjiang—are usually crowded and sparsely furnished. Students sit two and sometimes three to a desk. Children and teachers have a blackboard to work with and not much else. Books are in short supply, and there are no educational tools—maps, overhead projectors, computers—that aid learning in American schools.

But education is an intensely serious business everywhere in China. Children know from an early age that their record in school will determine the kind of work they will do as adults. Jobs are assigned to young people by the government, and only those who have gone past high school and done well in college have a chance for interesting and well-paying jobs. Because of family poverty and school fees, however,

A Uighur family in Kashgar. The electric lamp, radio, and rugs indicate that the family is rather well-to-do.

Students in a Turpan classroom.

only 50 percent of students in China complete middle school and only one out of ten graduates from high school.

Uighurs are no longer the most numerous ethnic group in Xinjiang Province. For over thirty years the Chinese Communist central government has encouraged and sometimes forced Han Chinese to migrate to Xinjiang until they now outnumber Uighurs. Han have come as government officials, office workers, teachers, soldiers, and farmers — to name but some of the roles they play in Xinjiang.

The Chinese government has promoted this migration not only for the purpose of developing Xinjiang but also because of Chinese concern about a Uighur desire for independence that burns as fiercely as it ever has in the past. Because of their historical origins in the Middle East, their Turkic language, their Muslim religion, and their belief in a free-

A Kazakh grandfather with his grandson.

market system rather than Communist controls, Uighurs have little in common with the Han Chinese. They are much closer to the people of Soviet Central Asia. They would like to have their own independent country, just as many of the ethnic culture groups of the Soviet Union clamor for their independence today. Uighur resentment of the Chinese has been especially deep since the 1966–76 Cultural Revolution. During those years the militant Chinese Red Guard forcibly suppressed Muslim practices, burned mosques, and put religious leaders in prison.

The Chinese government now forbids such harsh acts, but this has done nothing to reduce Uighur desire for their own government. At least seven resistance groups exist among the Uighurs, and riots against the Chinese have taken place in Kashgar and other Xinjiang cities in recent years. Because of these disturbances, Kashgar was again closed to all foreigners in 1990.

The Chinese have no intention of relaxing their hold on this region which serves as a buffer to the Soviet Union and has immense oil reserves. The Chinese army maintains sixteen divisions, about 130,000 men, in the military district that includes Xinjiang and keeps tight control over the area.

Because of their fear of reprisals, Uighur outbreaks of violence are rare, and the possibility of a successful separatist movement now or in the foreseeable future seems extremely remote. An uneasy peace prevails, but the tension that lies beneath the surface is real. In 1990 the *Washington Post* reported a Xinjiang militant as saying, "If people fight the Chinese, I like that. If I die . . . I'm very happy because Xinjiang is Turkestan, not China."

When journalists call Xinjiang "China's Wild West," they usually are referring to the smouldering conflict between the Uighurs and Han Chinese.

The market in Kashgar.

SIX

Kashgar

Paul, David, and Peter reached Kashgar by way of a three-hour flight from Urumqi in an aged turboprop plane. They were grateful for good weather because flights between Urumqi and Kashgar have been known to be delayed for as much as three days by savage sandstorms that arise from the Taklamakan Desert.

Their best view of the Taklamakan during the entire trip came from the air on this flight. They could see its immensity and starkness in a way they had been unable to in the train that clung to the desert's edge. They passed over a river that rose suddenly out of the desert, flowed for a short distance through the barren wasteland, then just as suddenly disappeared into the sand. No vegetation grew along this river; only brownish-white sand formed its edges. It was truly a "lost river" that began nowhere and ended nowhere.

In the old section of Kashgar near one of the many mosques.

The pilot brought the aircraft smoothly into Kashgar and deposited his passengers in a city that was old when Marco Polo stopped there to rest after his caravan's exhausting descent from the Pamir Mountains. Polo called Kashgar the biggest and "most splendid" city in the province and commented on the fine orchards, vineyards, and fields of cotton. He said that the inhabitants of Kashgar lived by "trade and industry" and noted that the city was the starting point for merchants who were going to market their wares all over the world.

Kashgar sits on the western edge of the Taklamakan Desert, and mountains with peaks rising over twenty thousand feet surround it on the three other sides. Five hundred years have passed since caravans plied the Silk Road, making their indispensable stop at this remote desert city. Yet today Kashgar has a population of 200,000, 80 percent of whom are Uighurs, and it has never lost its vitality as a Central Asian agricultural and trading city.

A modern crust has formed around old Kashgar: office buildings, bank, movie theater, apartments, housing blocks; but in the old city, the heart of which is called Yumlakshakulbishe, Uighur life still moves at the same pace and with the same rhythms that it has for centuries.

The first time Paul ventured into the old city, he could not shake the feeling that he was walking through the pages of the *Arabian Nights*. He was quickly lost in a maze of dusty alleyways. Donkey carts seemed to be almost the only form of transportation. The walls of the buildings along the alleys were all of adobe brick, some whitewashed, some long in need of repair. Behind these walls were the small courtyard homes where Uighur families have lived for hundreds of years.

While Marco Polo spoke well of Kashgar as a city, he had no such high opinion of the people who lived there. "The folk here are very close-fisted," he wrote, "and live very poorly, neither eating well nor drinking well." After roaming old Kashgar for only a short while, the Conklins concluded that either Polo had been in a bad mood when he visited the city or the Uighur people had become much more friendly and generous over the last five centuries. Wandering by himself, as years as a photographer have taught him to do, Paul was invited into several Uighur homes behind the alley walls. They were all the same, two rooms and a small courtyard. During each visit Paul was offered a bowl of cool yogurt and a piece of unleavened bread, like a small pita loaf. His cameras were welcome in every home.

On Peter's first walk down one of the dusty, unpaved streets, a young Uighur man, a total stranger, stopped him and invited him to a wedding reception that evening. David and Peter discovered an eating

All kinds of vehicles share this road leading into Kashgar.

place run by a Uighur man in his twenties who told them proudly that his cafe was "American style." The food wasn't American except for bagels with the Chinese equivalent of cream cheese, but from opening until closing he played American music on a cassette player. He had a dozen or so tapes that people passing through had left with him; the music was off-key as a result of the tapes having been badly stretched from overuse, but there was no doubt that it was American music.

"I sat there eating a bagel and listening to Jackson Browne singing off-key," Peter said. "It was the only American music I heard in China, and it sounded awfully good."

The main Kashgar bazaar is located on a long street in the old section. On each side of the street scores of merchants sit patiently in their stalls offering every kind of merchandise; in other stalls artisans make shoes, clothes, belts, knives, and other necessities of everyday life. Open-air cafes offering tea, coffee, and food dot the length of the street.

But Kashgar's grand moment comes on Sunday. This is the day of the great market, which, with one brief interruption, has been held in a large field outside the city for as many years as anyone can remember. The Sunday market was shut down for a few years during the Chinese Communist Cultural Revolution, which began in 1966. Among other things, the Cultural Revolution sought to totally prohibit free enterprise and impose the tightest government control over the economy. But even during those years, the Uighurs, for whom trading is almost like breathing, found ways and places to keep buying and selling their goods on a private, nongovernment-controlled basis.

In the late 1970s the government again changed its position and began to encourage entrepreneurship and private enterprise. The Kash-

Scene at the Kashgar market.

gar market quickly burst back into life, and today flourishes in — what seems to an outsider — a vast confusion of people, animals, dust, color, noise, and smells.

As Sunday dawns, families in donkey carts begin to arrive from small oasis towns and villages around Kashgar. The Soviet border is seventy-five miles from Kashgar; Afghanistan and Pakistan are within easy traveling distance. Eager merchants have always found a way to cross the borders; every Sunday traders from these countries are at the great Kashgar market to sell their wares and buy goods to take back. No one has ever been able to count the number of people who come

A section of the Sunday market is given over to second-hand shoes.

A Uighur merchant and his daughter.

An alley in old Kashgar. Donkey carts do most of the hauling here.

to the market, but estimates vary between 70,000 and 100,000 every Sunday.

This market is not meant for tourists but rather for local consumers and traders. Whole sections are devoted to knives, pots, hardware, lumber. Other sections contain large sacks of dried fruit, huge piles of woven mats, window frames, studded doors, fur hats, clothes of every description. In an especially colorful part of the market, textiles from all over Asia and Europe are on display; crowds of women examine and compare them with great interest.

Hungry eaters jam a profusion of outdoor restaurants throughout the day. The aromas of roasting mutton and baking bread mingle in the air with the smoke from a hundred cooking fires. The enormous animal market is filled with dust and noise as wary buyers inspect sheep, goats, camels, donkeys, and bullocks. In a large corral the dust and noise are even greater as eager young Kazakh riders try out horses, looking for just the right one to make them invincible in a game of *buz kashi*.

Like all visitors to Kashgar, David looked forward to the Sunday market as a highlight of the trip. "I had planned to spend the entire day," he said, "and I got there early. But after only four hours, I felt like I had spent my whole life there. The sheer intensity of it just drains your energy. Camels, rats, old worn-out shoes, herbs, medicine, jade, animal intestines, blocks of salt, rugs—it would take a week just to count the kinds of things that are for sale. Uighur children learn to be traders even before they're old enough to go to school. One boy about six years old was selling a silver-inlaid dagger to one of the few Americans in the market besides us. The only English he knew was, 'How much you pay?' But he knew how to use a pocket calculator, and with his few words and that tool, he made his sale. The boy's father was in

Buying a camel at the Kashgar Sunday market. This is serious business that can take a long time.

the background, just looking on. He didn't say anything, but he looked pleased with his son's performance."

Paul spent a few minutes watching two men haggling over the price of a camel. The owner demonstrated what a fine beast he was selling while the prospective buyer pointed out the animal's defects. The bargaining was good-natured, but there was no doubt of its seriousness. When Paul passed by an hour later the bargaining was still going on.

As he watched the continuing session, Paul recalled that Marco Polo and his father had bought fresh camels in Kashgar for their caravan. Paul wondered if the young Venetian might have formed his opinion of Uighurs as "close-fisted" in a camel-purchasing session on this very spot.

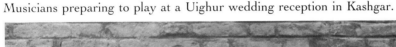
Musicians preparing to play at a Uighur wedding reception in Kashgar.

If Marco Polo returned today he might be puzzled by the bicycle in the background, but he would have no trouble recognizing this spoon merchant in the Kashgar market.

Land of Yesterday, Land of Tomorrow

A number of times on their journey through Xinjiang, Paul had the same thought: I have stepped into a time machine. If Marco Polo were standing beside me right now, he would recognize everything. Paul might have been looking at a trader leading his camel into the Kashgar market, listening to the muezzin calling the faithful to prayer at a mosque in Turpan, eating a slice of melon in the cool, shaded courtyard of a Uighur home, or feeling the excitement of a team of Kazakh horsemen as they fought for a sheep carcass in a game of *buz kashi*. Paul was sure that many of the sights, sounds, and rhythms of Xinjiang he was experiencing in the late twentieth century were virtually the same as they had been when Marco Polo reached Kashgar in 1275.

In many ways time has seemed to stand still in the oases and nomad camps of Chinese Central Asia. But what seems real and what is truly real are often different. The winds of change are blowing in Xinjiang and will continue to blow until they reach the force of the *kara-buran*, the black hurricane that drives the sands of the Taklamakan Desert.

Part of the change will be brought by the recent opening of the Karakoram Highway to foreign travelers. This highway is a spectacular engineering feat, a 766-mile road that runs from Kashgar across the Himalaya Mountains to Islamabad, the capital of Pakistan. The building of the Karakoram Highway took eighteen years of hard labor by Chinese and Pakistan army crews. The border is still tightly controlled, but in time the new highway will open up a dramatic increase of new trade between the two countries and bring an estimated twenty thousand additional visitors a year to Xinjiang.

But the greatest force for change in Xinjiang is oil. In only a few years over seventeen thousand Han Chinese have come from the heartland to work in the development of the oil industry. They have come as executives, petroleum engineers, geologists, drillers, refinery specialists, laborers, truck drivers. This is only the beginning; many thousands more and their families will follow. And industries based on petroleum, such as fertilizer factories, will grow up in Xinjiang.

Speaking of the importance of petroleum reserves in the Tarim Basin, an expert on oil in China at the Honolulu East-West Center recently said, "Tarim is absolutely critical to the economy. Tarim is their ticket to energy self-sufficiency."

To develop the Tarim Basin's oil potential a vast network of refineries, roads, bridges, and pipelines must be built. The cost will be enormous, and this infrastructure will take a long time to build. But it will come, and it will bring more changes to Xinjiang than few people living there now can imagine.

A modern office building encroaches on the old section of Kashgar.

A Chinese worker at the Karamay oil field in Xinjiang. The seventeen thousand Han who have already come from eastern China to help develop Xinjiang oil fields are only the beginning. Photograph by Lena H. Sun, courtesy *Washington Post*.

Water will continue to flow through the *karez* bringing life to the oases. Farmers will continue to grow melons, grain, grapes, and vegetables. The markets and bazaars will fight to hold their own against modern stores. But the time will come when Marco Polo, were he to again visit Xinjiang, would be puzzled by almost everything he might see.

80

Bibliography

Bonavia, Judy. *The Silk Road*. Secaucus, New Jersey: Chartwell Books, Inc., 1988.

Brophy, Gwenda. "China." *Population Today*, March, 1989.

Burns, John F. "In Marco Polo's Footsteps." *The New York Times*, June 22, 1986.

Fleming, Peter. *News from Tartary: A Journey from Peking to Kashmir*. Los Angeles: J. P. Tarcher, Inc., 1964. (Originally published by Charles Scribner's Sons, 1936).

Gibney, Frank, Jr. "Strangers in Their Own Land." *Newsweek*, October, 1, 1990.

Hopkirk, Peter. *Foreign Devils on the Silk Road*. Amherst: The University of Massachusetts Press, 1984.

Hucker, Charles O. *China's Imperial Past*. Stanford, California: Stanford University Press, 1975.

Kristof, Nicholas D. "In Rural China, Road to School Is All Uphill." *The New York Times*, December 3, 1990.

Major, John S. *The Land and People of China*. New York: J. B. Lippincott, 1989.

———.*The Land and People of Mongolia*. New York: J. B. Lippincott, 1990.

Oakes, Steven. "Outposts on China's Great Silk Road." *The New York Times*, June 22, 1986.

Polo, Marco. *The Travels of Marco Polo*. Harmondsworth, Middlesex, England: Penguin Books Ltd., 1958. (Translated with an introduction by Ronald Latham).

Rugoff, Milton. *Marco Polo's Adventures in China*. New York: American Heritage Publishing Company, Inc., 1964.

Stevens, Stuart. *Night Train to Turkistan*. New York: Atlantic Monthly Press, 1988.

Sun, Lena H. "Ancient Silk Road Oasis Restive." *The Washington Post*, September 25, 1990.

———."China Eyes Oil Field in Xinjiang." *The Washington Post*, October 9, 1990.

Tien, H. Yuan. "China: Demographic Billionaire." *Population Bulletin*, Vol. 38, No. 2, April, 1983. (Population Reference Bureau, Washington, D. C.)

Index

Afghanistan, 11, 69
Agricultural products, 36, 41–43, 64
Altai Mountains, 7, 10, 32
Animals
  camels, 10, 12, 15, 36, 74, 75
  goats, 10, 36, 51
  horses, 10, 16, 51, 54–55
  sheep, 10, 36, 51–52
  water buffalo, 5
Atacama Desert, 31
Autonomous regions, 6

Beijing, 13, 23, 24, 25
Bezelik monastery, 18–19
Buddhism, 18
Buddhist art, 18–19, 32
Buz kashi (Kazakh game), 51–52, 77

Caspian Sea, 6
Chicoine, Stephen, *xi*, 39
China trade, 3, 10, 15–17
China Travel Service, 13
Chinese Red Guard, 61
Communism, *x*, 53, 59, 61
Cultural Revolution, 61, 68

Daur, 53
Deserts
  as boundaries, 7
  Atacama, 31
  dangers of, 31–35

Gobi, 6, 7, 15, 23–24
Lop, 7
Taklamakan, 4, 10, 11, 15, 23–24,
  31–45, 47, 63–65, 78
Dunhuang, 15, 18, 23–24, 41

Education, 57, 58, 59

Flaming Mountains, 18, 33
Foods, 14, 30, 43, 44, 45, 51, 65, 68

Gansu Province, 5, 13, 24
Gobi Desert, 6, 7, 15, 23–24
Great Wall of China, 5, 15, 16

Han Chinese, 3, 5, 9, 10, 46, 53, 59,
  61, 78, 80
Heavenly Mountains. *See* Tian Shan
Hedin, Sven, 31
Himalaya Mountains, 78

India, 3, 14, 18
Inner Mongolia Autonomous Region,
  6
Irrigation. *See Karez*
Islam, 3, 18, 53, 56, 57, 59, 61, 77

Japan, 19
Jiayuguan Fortress, 15, 16

Kara-buran (sandstorm), 32–33, 78
Karakoram Highway, 78
Karakoram Mountains, 32
Karez (irrigation tunnels), 38, 39, 42, 47, 51
Kashgar, 4, 15, 23, 24, 26, 27, 28, 32, 34, 37, 56, 58, 63–75, 76, 77, 79
Kazakh, 10, 49, 50, 51–53, 54–55, 56, 60, 73, 77
Kirghiz, 10, 53, 56
Korea, 19
Kunlun Mountains, 7, 10, 11, 32

Loess, 24, 25
Lop Desert, 7

Magao Caves, 18–19, 20–21
Mongolia, 53
Mongols, 4, 53
Mountains
    Altai, 7, 10, 32
    as boundaries, 7
    Flaming, 18, 33
    Himalaya, 78
    Karakoram range, 32
    Kunlun range, 7, 10, 11, 32
    Pamir, 7, 10, 64
    Tian Shan, 7, 10, 15, 50, 51
Muslims. *See* Islam

Nomads. *See* Kazakh and Kirghiz
North China Plain, 5

Oases, 3, 15, 18, 30, 32, 33, 35–38, 40, 41–43, 45, 47, 57, 69, 77

Pakistan, 11, 69, 78
Pamir Mountains, 7, 10, 64

People's Republic of China
    area, 5
    boundaries, 4–5
    defense of, 11, 35, 61
    economy, 11
Persia, 3, 14, 34, 38
Petroleum, 11, 33, 61, 78, 80
Photography, *ix–x, xi,* 22, 24, 26–27, 28, 29
Polo, Marco, 4, 33–35, 43, 45, 64, 65, 75, 76, 77, 80

Silk, 17
Silk Road, 3, 12, 13–19, 23, 27, 33–34, 64
Smithsonian Institution Associates, *x,* 13
Soviet Union, 4, 11, 61, 69
Sykes, Sir Percy, 31

Tajik, 53
Taklamakan Desert, 4, 10, 11, 15, 23–24, 31–45, 47, 63–65, 78
Tarim Basin, 11, 78
Tian Shan, 7, 10, 15, 50, 51
Tibet Autonomous Region, 6
Tibetan Plateau, 5, 7
Train travel, 13–15
Travels of Marco Polo, The, 34
Turkestan, 6, 53
Turkic languages, 3, 6, 10, 31, 59
Turpan, 18, 29, 37, 40, 41–42, 47–48, 77

Uighurs, 7, 8, 10, 53, 57, 58, 59, 61, 65, 68, 71, 73, 75, 77
Urumqi, 26, 35, 37, 63

Von Richtofen, Ferdinand, 17

Women, *7, 23, 27, 55*

Xian, *13, 15, 32*
Xibe, *53*
Xinjiang Uighur Autonomous
    Region
  boundaries, *6–7, 11*
  Chinese control of, *53, 59, 61*

economy, *78*
ethnic groups, *10, 53, 59*
language, *10, 57*
population, *10*
schools, *57*

Yellow Sea, *5*